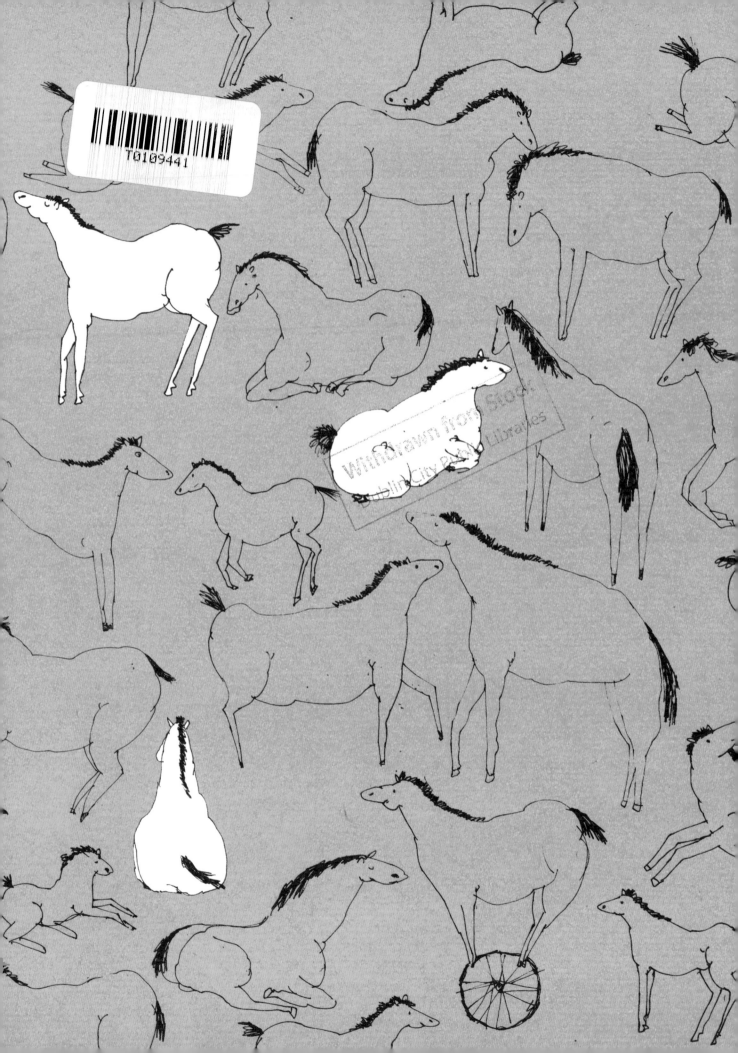

In the Meadow of Fantasies

HADI MOHAMMADI

In the Meadow of Fantasies

ILLUSTRATED BY
Nooshin Safakhoo

Translated from the Persian by
Sara Khalili

elsewhere
editions

There was one,   one horse.
Then there were two,   two horses.
Then there were three,   three horses.
Then there were four,   four horses.
Then there were five,   five horses.
Then there were six,   six horses.
Then there were seven,   seven horses.

The young girl murmured
as she gazed at the meadow
through the window of her fantasies.

The seven horses were and were not of seven colors.

The first horse was white.

The second horse was black.

The third horse was red.

The fourth horse was yellow.

The fifth horse was grey.

The sixth horse was brown.

But the seventh horse had no color at all.

The other horses each gave a patch of their color
to the colorless horse.

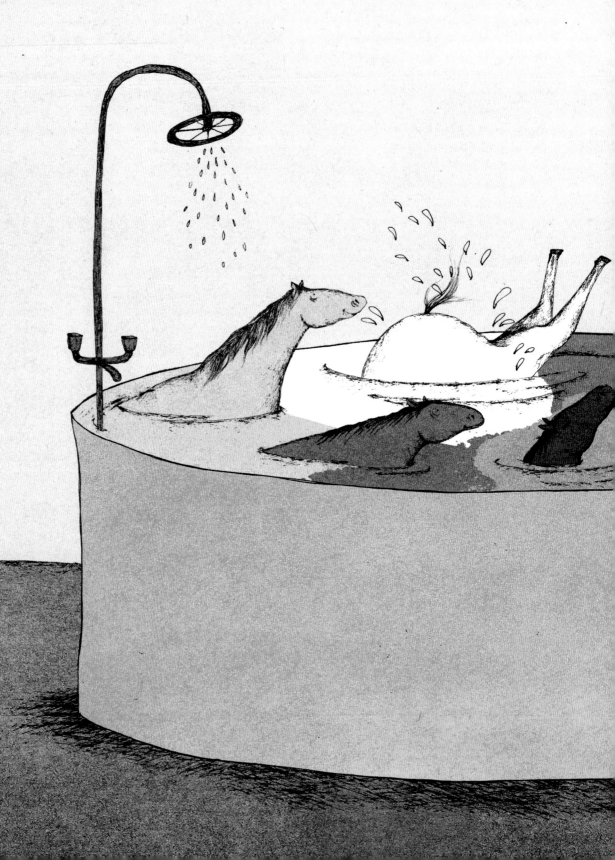

Now the seventh horse
was of every color.

The seven horses had and did not have seven homes of their own.

The first horse lived in a great valley.
The second horse lived in a forest.
The third horse lived in a meadow.
The fourth horse lived in a desert.
The fifth horse lived on the seashore.

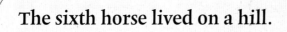

The sixth horse lived on a hill.

But the seventh horse had no home of its own.

The other horses each gave part of their home to
the seventh horse.
Now the seventh horse had a home everywhere.

They were seven horses that had and did not have
   seven dreams and fantasies.

The first horse fancied itself the fastest steed on the planet.
The second horse fell in love with a tree that cast the broadest shade.
The third horse's world became a stream teeming with fish,
   large and small.

The fourth horse dreamed of nothing but moons and stars.
The fifth horse created a lush, green universe for itself.
The sixth horse daydreamed of a young girl gazing at it
   through the window of her fantasies.
The young girl read the sixth horse's mind
   and a smile spread across her lips.

She wondered, What *about the seventh horse?*
   Why does it not have any dreams?

The young girl had hardly finished her thought when the other
horses gathered together some of their visions and dreams,
and offered them to the seventh horse.

Now the seventh horse's mind was full of beautiful flights of fantasy.

They were seven horses with seven foals.
The first horse's foal was only one week old.
The second horse's foal was two weeks old.
The third horse's foal was three weeks old.
The fourth horse's foal was four weeks old.
The fifth horse's foal was five weeks old.
The sixth horse's foal was six weeks old.

But the seventh horse's foal was not even seven days old.

It was just a day old.

A newborn.

The other horses celebrated the birth of the newborn foal.
A celebration with songs of moonlight and blossoms,
of milk for the newborn to suckle and grow.

Seven weeks of seven days passed.

The seven foals were growing.
The youngest foal was seven weeks old,
the oldest foal was two times seven weeks old.

Seven weeks passed, and then seven months.

The seven foals had grown.
They were seven horses of seven colors,
but one was of more than one color.

They were seven horses with seven homes of their own,
but one had more than one home of its own.

They were seven horses with seven dreams,

but one had more than one dream.

The time had come for the horses to return.

The horse of more than one color,
the horse with more than one home of its own,
the horse that had more than one dream,
galloped as fast as lightning until it reached the window
of the young girl's fantasies.

The horse of more than one color,
the horse with more than one home
    of its own,
the horse with more than one dream,
shared its colors with the young girl,
shared its homes with the young girl,
shared its flights of fantasy with the
    young girl.

The young girl beamed with joy.
She looked at the horse of seven
    colors and asked,
"Shall we together write the story
    of *Seven Nights and Seven Moons?*"

I ALWAYS WANTED TO BE A CROW instead of a human. That's why in most social media sites my profile picture is a crow. I've also written stories about crows and found inspiration through them. In other words, there's an inner crow living inside me. Sometimes when I become too wise, it reminds me, *You're a crow, you shouldn't plant your feet too firmly on the ground.*

I wrote with my left hand, and when I started school, we had a penmanship teacher who hated left handed people. My handwriting was bad, and every chance he got, he would put a pencil between my fingers and squeeze. When I was thirteen, I wrote a composition, and this time, a teacher I really liked predicted that I would become a writer. My youth passed in the chaos of revolution, grueling and merciless. For forty years I've been writing and laying my head down to sleep with the hope for freedom. But if I die without freedom, remember that my pen wrote for the love of freedom.

—HADI MOHAMMADI

MY BEST CHILDHOOD PLAYMATE was my father. Sometimes we were a lion and his cub, other times a large ship that harbored a little boat inside it. Yet, the best time we spent together was when he told me stories and I simultaneously drew them. Stories he had made up of real-life characters, but with strange names and behaviors, who went about common daily routines in uncommon ways. To me, he is still the greatest storyteller and I wish to tell stories to children by drawing them as sweetly as he narrated them.

—NOOSHIN SAFAKHOO

I GREW UP IN A HOME WITH NO TELEVISION. My father called it the idiocy box and refused to allow one in the house. He wanted us to read instead. When I was too young to read, my entertainment was the Persian folk tales Naneh Kobi used to tell me. In reality, my nanny was as engaging as her folk tales. She was funny and eccentric, and always dressed in her tribal Qashqai clothes—colorful embroidered shirts and long multi-layered skirts hemmed with ribbons. Now and then she would drift off in the middle of a story and I, nestled on her lap, would tug at her sequined headscarf pinned under her chin to bring her back. When I was a little older, Naneh Kobi went back to her tribe and amazing pop-up and picture books replaced her stories. Other books for other ages followed. Decades have since passed and my love of stories and books continues. I always think of my father, and I often wish I had a photograph of Naneh Kobi.

—SARA KHALILI

Originally published as هفت اسب هفت رنگ (Haft Asb Haft Rang)
by The Institute for Research on the History of Children's Literature,
Tehran, Iran in 2017.
Copyright text © Hadi Mohammadi, 2018
Copyright illustrations © Nooshin Safakhoo, 2014
English language translation © Sara Khalili, 2021
First Elsewhere Edition, 2021

Also published as *Het meisje en haar zeven paarden* by
Em. Querido's Uitgeverij, Amsterdam in 2018.

Design by Gopa & Ted2, Inc.

ISBN 978-1-939810-90-8
Library of Congress Cataloging-in-Publication Data available upon request.

Elsewhere Editions
232 3rd Street #A111
Brooklyn, NY 11215
www.elsewhereeditions.org

Distributed by Penguin Random House
www.penguinrandomhouse.com

This work was made possible by the New York State Council on the Arts with the
support of Governor Andrew M. Cuomo and the New York State Legislature.

Funding for the translation of this book was provided by a grant from the
Carl Lesnor Family Foundation.

Archipelago Books also gratefully acknowledges the generous support of
Lannan Foundation, Nimick Forbesway Foundation, the National Endowment
for the Arts, and the New York City Department of Cultural Affairs.

PRINTED IN CHINA

*elsewhere
editions*

Elsewhere Editions, an imprint of Archipelago Books, is devoted
to translating luminous works of children's literature
from around the world.
www.elsewhereeditions.org

and the Pooka fell asleep.
It wasn't lonely anymore.
(It was busy planning the next party!)

Shona Shirley Macdonald is a Scottish author/illustrator based in County Waterford. Her projects range from publications of poetry and fiction to concept artwork for theatre. She also illustrates greeting cards and T-shirts for her design company Mireog. Her work has been exhibited nationally and internationally.

Her artwork for *The Moon Spun Round: W.B. Yeats for Children*, edited by Noreen Doody, was described as 'breathtaking', 'magical' and 'reminiscent of Clark, Rackham and PJ Lynch'.

'Mysterious and beautiful illustrations spin out from Yeats's haunting and enchanted words and rhythms, bringing the spirit and beauty of his writing in this collection to a whole new audience.'
Primary Times

'Gossamer-light drawings dance around the text like a wave on the sea … will enchant readers of all ages and open many eyes to the beauty of the poetry.'
Evening Echo

'Absolutely gorgeous.' Eithne Shortall,
Sunday Times

'Faery worlds and faery creatures come to life through the colourful illustrations and will instantly appeal to children.'
Seomra Ranga

First published 2017 by The O'Brien Press Ltd,
12 Terenure Road East, Rathgar, Dublin 6, D06 HD27, Ireland
Tel: +353 1 4923333; Fax: +353 1 4922777
E-mail: books@obrien.ie
Website: www.obrien.ie
The O'Brien Press is a member of Publishing Ireland.

ISBN: 978-1-78849-000-9

6 5 4 3 2 1
20 19 18

Printed and bound by Gutenberg Press, Malta.
The paper in this book is produced using pulp from managed forests.

Published in

DUBLIN
UNESCO
City of Literature